GOODNIGHT
LULU

Paulette Bogan

BLOOMSBURY
CHILDREN'S
BOOKS

Type set in Maiandra
The art was done in watercolor and inks
Designed by Marikka Tamura

Published by Bloomsbury, New York and London
Distributed to the trade by St. Martin's Press
Library of Congress Cataloging-in-Publication Data
Bogan, Paulette. Goodnight Lulu/by Paulette Bogan. p. cm.
Summary: When her mother tucks her in for the night, Lulu the chicken
worries what would happen if a bear of a tiger or an alligator
should come in during the night.
[1. Chickens—Fiction. 2. Bedtime—Fiction. 3. Mother and child—Fiction.]
I. Title.   PZ7.B6339 Go 2003   {E} 21 2002027825   CIP
ISBN 1-58234-803-0

3 5 7 9 10 8 6 4
Printed in Dubai

Bloomsbury USA Children's Books
175 Fifth Avenue
New York, NY 10010

To my little chickadee, Lulu...
My pookie bear, Sophia...
My sweetie pie, Rachael...
And my schnookie, Charlie!

Lulu climbed into her bed. Her momma tucked her in, fluffed her hay and pecked her on the head... gently of course.

"Goodnight, my little chickadee," said Momma.
"Goodnight, my momma," said Lulu.

As Momma Chicken turned out the lights,
Lulu called out, "What if a big, brown
bear comes in while I am sleeping?"
"Oh sweetie, there are no bears here," said Momma.
"But what if there IS a bear?" asked Lulu.

"Then I would flap and cluck and scare it and chase it all the way back to the forest where it belongs!" answered Momma.
Lulu smiled.

"Goodnight now, my sweetie pie," whispered Momma.

"Momma?" asked Lulu.

"Yes, Lulu," said Momma.

"What if a big, striped tiger comes in while
I am sleeping?" asked Lulu.

"Oh honey, there are no tigers here," said Momma.

"But what if there IS a tiger?" asked Lulu.

"Then I would pull its tail and roar and drag that tiger all the way back to the jungle where it belongs!" answered Momma.
Lulu giggled.

"Goodnight now, my little pumpkin," said Momma.

"But MOMMA, what if an alligator comes in while
I am sleeping?" asked Lulu.

"Oh my little pookie bear, there are NO alligators here,"
answered Momma.

"But what if there IS an alligator?" asked Lulu.

"Then I would stomp and yell and chase it all the way back to the icky, sticky swamp where it belongs!" answered Momma.

Lulu's eyes were getting sleepy.

Lulu sat up one more time with a smile on her face. "Momma, what if the pigs come in while I am sleeping?"

Momma turned back to look at Lulu.
"Oh my little darling, did you say,
what if the PIGS come in while
you are sleeping?"
Lulu's eyes widened.

"Then I would grab them and tickle them and squeeze them and kiss them all over their faces!"

"And then I would tuck them in and say goodnight."
So Momma Chicken did just that.

Lulu and the pigs were all comfy, cozy now
and almost asleep when Lulu said,
"Momma?"
"Yes, my love?" sighed Momma.

"I love you, Momma!" laughed Lulu.
And Momma answered,
"Goodnight, my little Lulu,
I love you, too."